HELPING YOUR BRAND-NEW READER

Here's how to make first-time reading easy and fun:

◗ Read the introduction at the beginning of each story aloud. Look through the pictures together so that your child can see what happens in the story before reading the words.

◗ Read one or two pages to your child, placing your finger under each word.

◗ Let your child touch the words and read the rest of the story. Give him or her time to figure out each new word.

◗ If your child gets stuck on a word, you might say, *"Try something. Look at the picture. What would make sense?"*

◗ If your child is still stuck, supply the right word. This will allow him or her to continue to read and enjoy the story. You might say, *"Could this word be 'ball'?"*

◗ Always praise your child. Praise what he or she reads correctly, and praise good tries too.

◗ Give your child lots of chances to read the story again and again. The more your child reads, the more confident he or she will become.

◗ Have fun!

Text copyright © 2010 by David Martin
Illustrations copyright © 2010 by Akemi Gutierrez

First edition 2010

Library of Congress Cataloging-in-Publication Data is available.
Library of Congress Catalog Card Number 2009032481
ISBN 978-0-7636-4068-2

09 10 11 12 13 14 SWT 10 9 8 7 6 5 4 3 2 1

Printed in Dongguan, Guangdong, China

This book was typeset in Letraset Arta.
The illustrations were done in watercolor and ink.

Candlewick Press
99 Dover Street
Somerville, Massachusetts 02144

visit us at www.candlewick.com

Three
Little Bears
Play All Day

CANDLEWICK PRESS

David Martin ILLUSTRATED BY **Akemi Gutierrez**

Contents

THREE LITTLE BEARS JUMP

1

Introduction

This story is called *Three Little Bears Jump.* It's about how Sister Bear, Brother Bear, and Baby Bear jump and spin. Then Baby Bear spins and spins until he's dizzy.

3

Brother Bear jumps.

Brother Bear spins.

Sister Bear jumps.

Sister Bear spins.

Baby Bear jumps.

Baby Bear spins.

Baby Bear spins and spins and spins!

"I'm dizzy," says Baby Bear.

THREE LITTLE BEARS JUGGLE

Introduction

This story is called *Three Little Bears Juggle*.
It's about how Brother Bear has apples and
Sister Bear has bananas, and they can juggle
them. Then Baby Bear juggles pies.

13

Brother Bear has apples.

Brother Bear juggles the apples.

Sister Bear has bananas.

Sister Bear juggles the bananas.

The bears eat the apples and bananas.

Baby Bear has pies.

Baby Bear juggles the pies. Oops!

Baby Bear eats the pies.

THREE LITTLE BEARS EAT

Introduction

This story is called *Three Little Bears Eat*.
It's about how Brother Bear and Sister Bear
eat green food like peas and broccoli, but
Baby Bear says, "Green food is yucky!"
Then he tries mint ice cream.

Brother Bear and Sister Bear eat peas.

24

"Green food is yucky!" says Baby Bear.

25

Then they eat string beans.

"Green food is yucky!" says Baby Bear.

Then they eat broccoli.

"Green food is yucky!" says Baby Bear.

Then they eat mint ice cream.

30

"Green food is yummy!" says Baby Bear.

Introduction

This story is called *Three Little Bears Build.*
It's about how Brother Bear and Sister Bear
build a tower. They put a red block on the
tower and then put on other colored blocks
until — oh, no! Here comes Baby Bear!

Brother and Sister Bear build a tower.

34

They put a red block on the tower.

35

They put a blue block on the tower.

They put a yellow block on the tower.

They put a green block on the tower.

38

Oh, no! Here comes Baby Bear!

39

Oh, no! No tower.

They put a red block on Baby Bear.